FRED & Forest AND FRIENDS
AT THE
Hospital

Copyright © ticktock Entertainment Ltd 2007
First published in Great Britain in 2007 by ticktock Media Ltd.,
Unit 2, Orchard Business Centre, North Farm Road,
Tunbridge Wells, Kent, TN2 3XF

author: Melanie Joyce
ticktock project editor: Julia Adams
ticktock project designer: Emma Randall
ticktock image co-ordinator: Lizzie Knowles

We would like to thank: Colin Beer, Tim Bones, Rebecca Clunes, James Powell, Dr. Naima Browne, Claire O'Connor and the Monkton Ward staff at Maidstone Hospital, Senior Sister Caroline Stephenson and the staff on Kipling Ward at the Conquest Hospital Hastings, Mark Wadbrook and Paul Dine from Sussex Ambulance and Crowborough War Memorial Hospital

ISBN 978 1 84696 509 8 pbk

Printed in China

Picture credits

t=top b=bottom
All photography by Colin Beer of JL Allwo... ...com: 11r. Shutterstock: 22cl, 22tr, 23.

Every effort has been made to trace ... for any unintentional omissions.
We would be pleased to insert ... nt edition of this publication.

D0306368

Fred

Arthur

Meet Fred Bear and Friends

Betty

Jess

Poor Arthur has had an accident. He has fallen off his bike!

He has hurt his left arm and bumped his head. Arthur lies very still for several minutes.

When Arthur sits up he doesn't remember where he is. Fred is very worried. He dials 999 and asks for an ambulance.

The ambulance comes very quickly. Fred travels to hospital with Arthur.

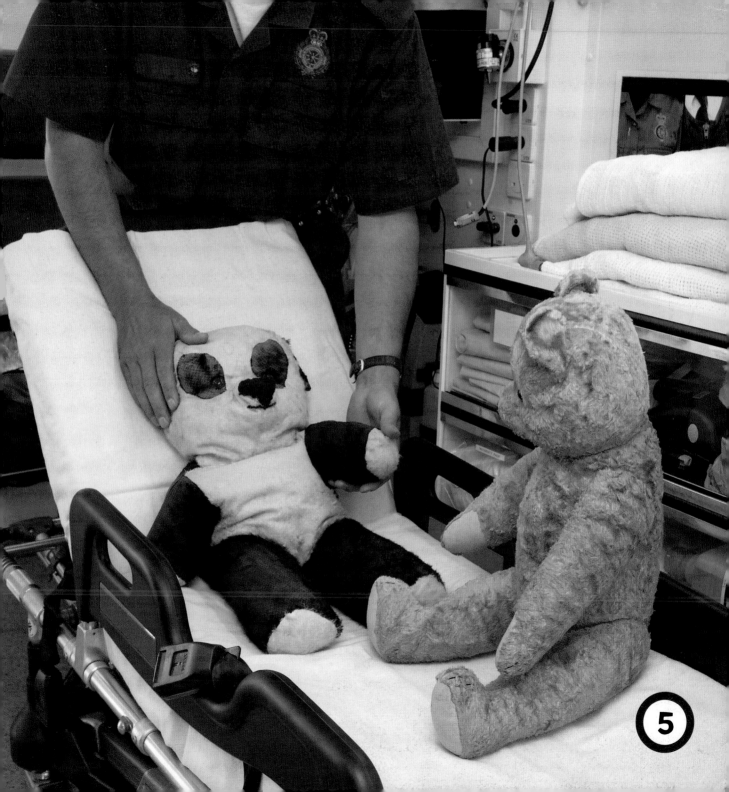

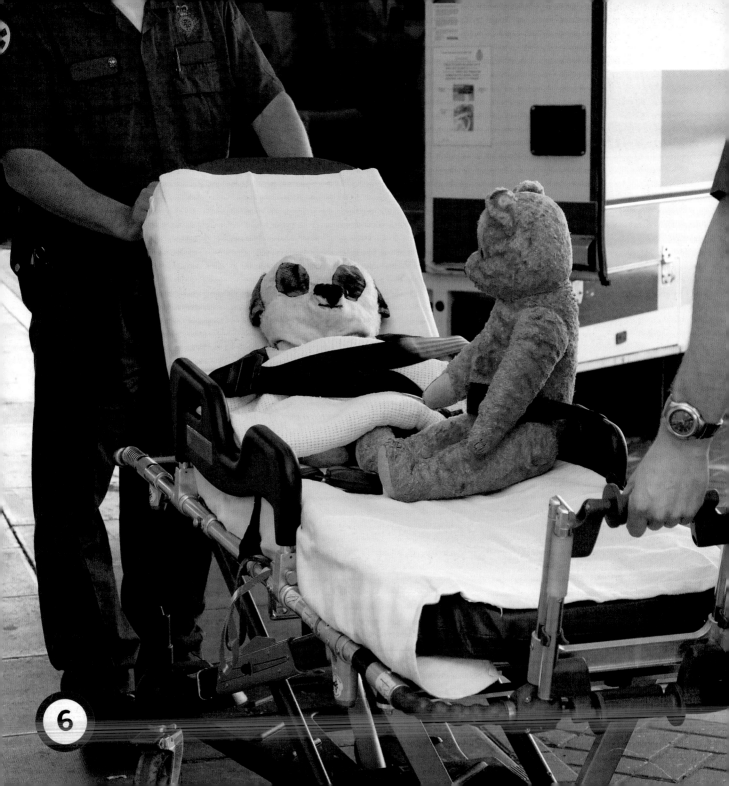

The ambulance drivers take Arthur to the Accident and Emergency Department at the hospital. Fred and Arthur sit in the waiting room.

Then a nurse calls Fred and Arthur: "The doctor is ready to see you," she says, "please follow me."

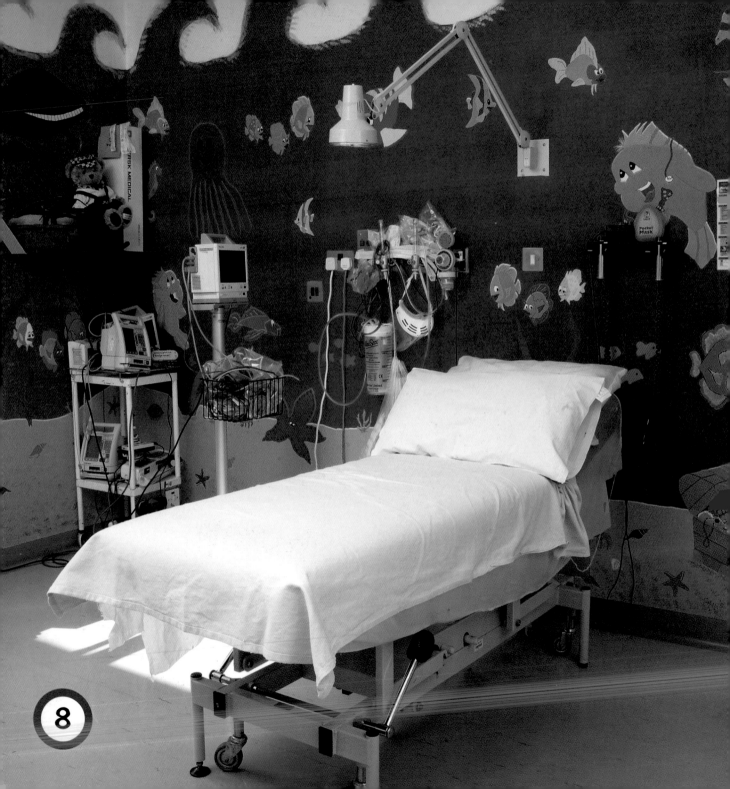

The nurse shows Arthur and Fred into a room and asks Arthur to lie on the bed.

The nurse says, "I think you will need to stay in hospital tonight. Because you are staying here for a while, you will need this name bracelet."

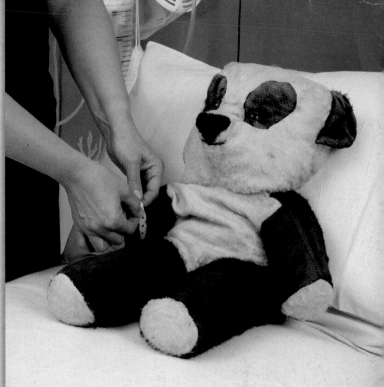

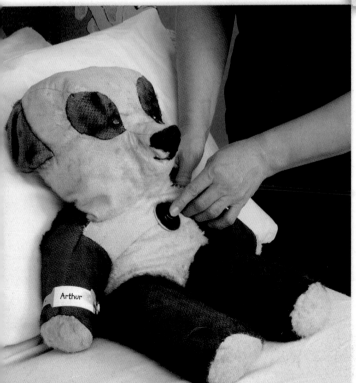

The doctor checks Arthur's eyes and then she listens to Arthur's heart:

'thump,
      thump.'

Then the doctor checks Arthur's arm. She says "You will need an x-ray."

9

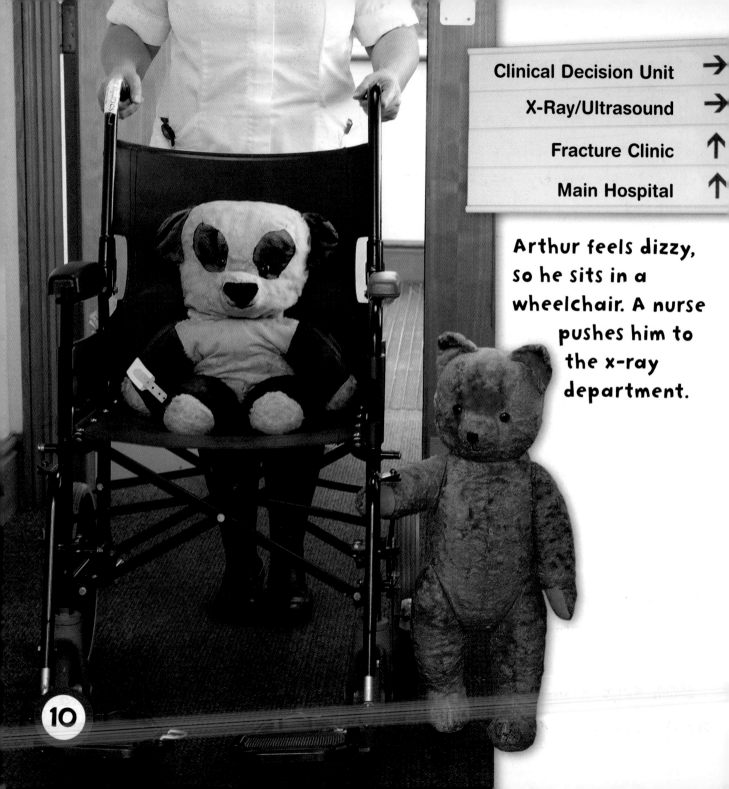

Clinical Decision Unit →

X-Ray/Ultrasound →

Fracture Clinic ↑

Main Hospital ↑

Arthur feels dizzy, so he sits in a wheelchair. A nurse pushes him to the x-ray department.

In the x-ray department,
a special machine takes
a picture of Arthur's arm.
The picture is called an
x-ray. It shows the doctor
what is inside Arthur's arm.

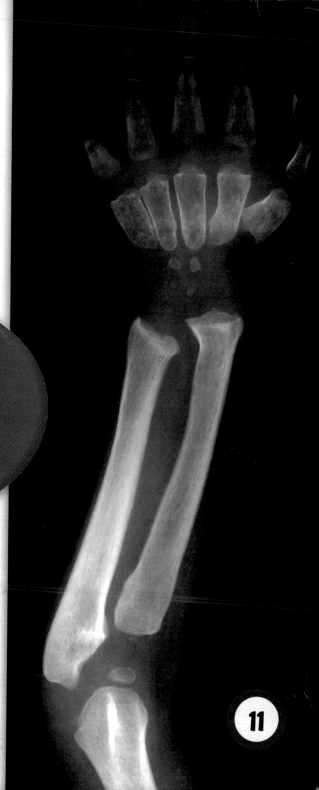

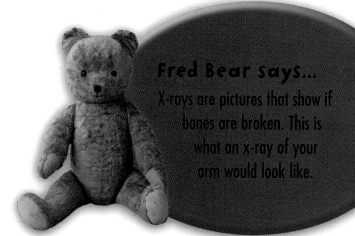

Fred Bear says...
X-rays are pictures that show if
bones are broken. This is
what an x-ray of your
arm would look like.

The doctor shows the x-ray
to Arthur and Fred.

"You are lucky," says the
doctor, "your arm is not broken."

Another nurse takes Arthur to a room. This is where Arthur will be staying tonight. He is very excited. The room has a lovely big bed.

Fred has to go home now.
He wants to tell Betty and
Jess that Arthur will be okay.

Fred says "Goodbye Arthur.
I will be back later."

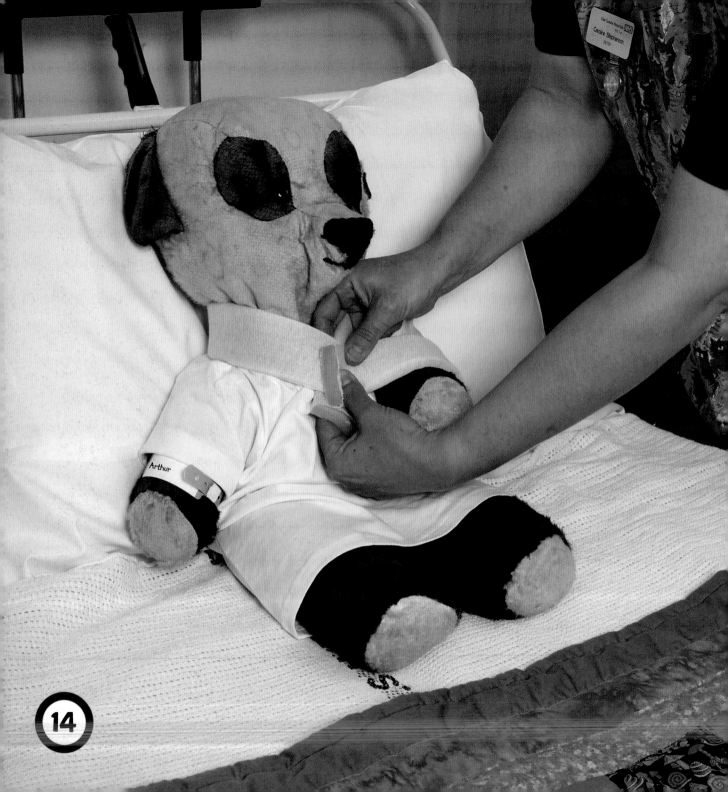

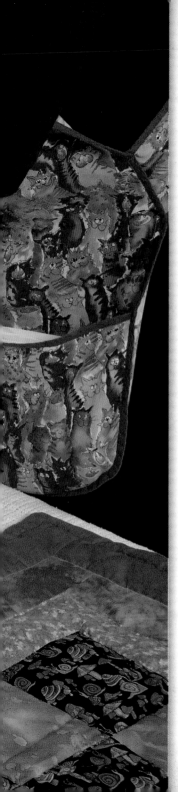

A nurse takes care of Arthur. She gives him a special gown to wear.

"My arm is still sore," says Arthur. The nurse puts Arthur's arm in a sling.

Then Fred comes back to the hospital. He has a present for Arthur.

Arthur is very happy that Fred has come to visit him. He is excited about the lovely balloon, too.

When Fred leaves,
Arthur has his dinner.

It has been a long day.
Arthur is very tired, so
he goes to sleep.

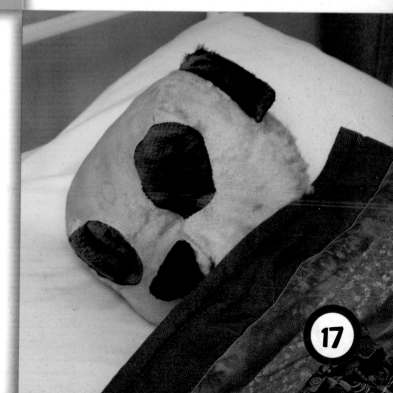

The next morning, the doctor checks Arthur's head and arm.

"You are well enough to go home now, Arthur," says the doctor.

The doctor tells Arthur to always wear a helmet on his bike. A helmet can protect Arthur's head.

Arthur and Fred go home in the car. Arthur holds on to his balloon tightly.

Get
Well
Soon!

19

Arthur's friends want to know all about the hospital. They play doctors and patients.

"Let me listen to your heart," says Doctor Betty.

Arthur is glad that there are hospitals to go to, but he thinks there is nothing nicer than coming home!

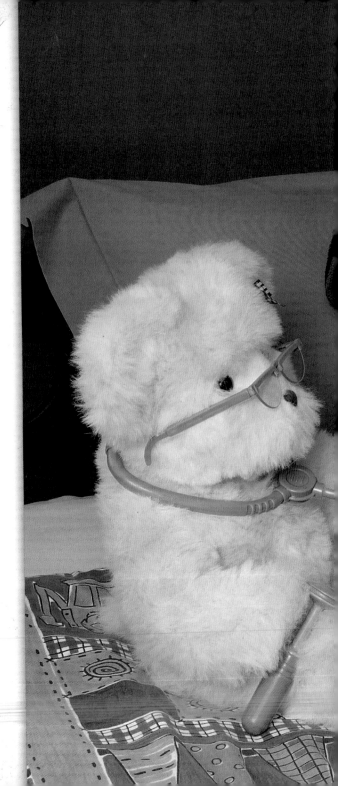

Accidents

Arthur had to go to the hospital because he had an accident. Fred says this is what you can do to stay safe:

Roads

Always wear your cycle helmet when you ride your bicycle.

When you cross the road, make sure you can see the green man. The red man means you have to wait.

Always wear a seatbelt when you are in a car.

Never play with
matches or lighters.
Fire is very dangerous.

Hot drinks can burn you.
Don't touch a cup if you
think it might be hot.

Can you think
of more ways
to stay safe?

Cleaning products can be
dangerous. Make sure you
never eat or drink them.

23

Parts of the Body

Look at these labels. Can you match them to Fred's body parts?

tummy

leg

eye

nose

head

arm

ear

mouth